God's Love is Like

Written and Illustrated by Ray Buckley

01 02 03 04 05 06 07 -- 10 9 8 7 6 5 4 3 2
MANUFACTURED IN HONG KONG

Abingdon Press
Nashville

Sarai Gets to See Jesus

he first thing Sarai (SAIR-eye) noticed about the man walking toward her with her abba (daddy) was that he was very tall. Sarai was a very small girl.

"Sarai," Abba said, "I want you to meet my friend, Jacob Bar-Jona. When we were boys, we played and learned together in the synagogue. Then Jacob and his family moved away. I missed him, but we see each other every year when we go to the Temple in Jerusalem. Now he has come to hear Jesus, just like we have."

Sarai tilted her head way back and looked up into the smiling face of her father's friend. Then she turned back to look for Jesus. She couldn't see him! There were legs everywhere. Big legs. Small legs. Fat legs. Skinny legs. Brown legs and pale legs. All Sarai could see was legs! She said as politely as she could, "Please, I can't see," but no one heard her. The legs didn't move.

Jesus was telling a story, but Sarai couldn't see him. She wanted to see Jesus. She pulled gently on a robe in front of her. "P-p-please, could I see?" No one answered, and the crowd grew even bigger. Sarai tried to find her way to the front of the crowd, but there were too many people.

Some people laughed

and wouldn't let her through. Some people didn't even notice her. She was about to cry when she heard a voice way up over her head. "Ah, Little One, let me help you." It was Abba's friend, Jacob Bar-Jona!

Two big hands lifted Sarai up, up, up above the legs — above the small, brown, and pale legs. They lifted her above the big and skinny legs. They lifted her up into the air and set her down in front of the crowd.

She saw the sun and the blue sky. She saw a large, beautiful tree. Under the tree was . . . Jesus!

Jesus said, "I want to tell you a story. There once was a man who was taking a trip. On the way, some robbers hurt him and took his money and clothes and left him all alone." Sarai knew how the man must have felt.

Jesus continued, "A priest saw the man who was hurt but ran to the other side of the road and pretended not to see him. A smart man, who had gone to school a long time, saw the man who was hurt but did not stop to help him." Sarai felt so sad for the hurt man. *She* would have tried to help him!

Jesus finished the story. "Another man came along the same road. He was different from many people in that country. Some people did not like him because he was different. He saw the hurt man lying by the side of the road. He fixed the man's cuts and took him to a place to rest until he could travel again."

Jesus looked at the crowd and asked, "Which of the people in my story was the best neighbor?" Sarai knew. It was the one who helped the hurt man — just like Jacob Bar-Jona had helped her to see Jesus. She turned to smile at Jacob Bar-Jona and Abba. Sarai had seen Jesus and had met a wonderful neighbor all in the same day. She felt very happy and very *tall*.

The Little Seed That Grew

There once was a tiny mustard seed. It was so small that it was even smaller than the small seeds. It was so small that the man who sold seeds said, "This seed is too small. It will never amount to anything!" And he brushed the seed off of his hands.

A farmer's wife was hurrying by. The tiny seed landed on her sleeve. It was so small she didn't see it. Later, when she was making bread for her family, the seed fell off into the dough. It landed right on top of one of the loaves of bread.

At breakfast, when the farmer was eating his bread, he dropped a crumb of bread onto the table. The tiny seed was there, right on top. But it was so small he didn't see it.

After breakfast the farmer's wife gathered up the

tablecloth and shook the crumbs out of the window. A little mouse grabbed up the crumb and scurried away. A shadow passing overhead frightened him and he dropped the crumb on the ground and hid under a leaf. The shadow was a sparrow who swooped down to pick up the crumb. As the sparrow flew away, the tiny seed fell onto a flower with a wonderful smell.

A bee stopped to gather pollen from the flower and the seed stuck to his leg. While buzzing back to the hive with his load of pollen, the bee stopped to sting an old cow. When the cow swatted the bee with her tail, the seed fell to the ground. The cow did not see the little seed and stepped on it. The little seed went into the ground.

God blessed the tiny seed. It began to sprout! A small green shoot began to grow from the seed. A year passed. The little plant was a foot tall. Two years passed — it was four feet tall.

Winter after winter, summer after summer, the little plant grew. Finally, it was ten feet tall. The sparrow flew into it and built a nest.

The seed seller passed by and said, "What a

wonderful tree! Where did it come from?" The farmer exclaimed to his wife, "I wish we had a tree like that!" The bee built a hive in its branches, and the mouse found a place for a nest in its roots. The old cow came and stood in the shade from the tree when the day was hot.

Jesus said, "God's family is like the tiny mustard seed. It may seem tiny at first. But like the little seed, it sprouts and grows as big as a beautiful tree. Just like you!"

Keetah's Special Day

a-boom! Ka-boom! Ka-boom! The drums were starting. They sounded like thunder. *Today is a special day*, the drums seemed to say. Keetah tried to walk politely, but she wanted to jump and run. She was very happy.

Keetah's tribe, the Haida (HI-duh), make beautiful masks that they use for telling stories. First the masks are carved from wood. Then they are painted bright colors. Keetah knew she would see beautiful masks on this storytelling day.

Keetah felt small as she entered the community house. She looked at its posts that were made from the trunks of large trees. She saw a net filled with feathers stretched up high near the top of the room.

Keetah's grandmother wore a beautiful blanket. When all the people had gathered, she walked to the center of the room and said, "This is a story Jesus taught us. It is the story of the father who forgave."

The storytelling dancers took their places as Grandmother began: "Once there was a man who had two sons. One was older, and one was younger. The man loved his sons more than anything he owned. He was happy."

Keetah looked at the dancers. The beautiful masks they held looked like happy faces.

Grandmother continued quietly, "One day the younger son asked his father to give him the son's share of what the family owned. 'I want to visit places far away,' said the younger son. 'I don't want to live here anymore.'

"The young man went away and his father was sad. The young man spent all his money. Then he had nothing to eat. The only job he could find was feeding pigs."

Keetah looked at the dancers. They danced as if they were tired. The masks they held looked like sad faces. The story was almost over. Grandmother said, "The young man wanted to go home. He remembered how much his father loved him. He said, 'I would rather be a worker in my father's house than be alone and unhappy.'

"From a long way off the father saw his son coming. He was happy. He started walking, then running, then *running and running* to meet his son.

He hugged his son and shouted, 'Welcome home!' and the father forgave the son as if nothing bad had happened."

Keetah looked at the storytelling dancers. They were dancing very fast now and all their masks looked like smiling faces. They were happy like the father in the story.

Keetah's grandmother smiled and said, "God is like the father in Jesus' story. God loves us even when we are wrong. God forgives us and runs to meet us. At God's house we find only love."

Suddenly the net came loose and wonderful, beautiful feathers fell all about the people listening. Keetah picked up a happiness mask and held it tight. This day was special!

Jody Learns About Good Soil

orms! Red worms and brown worms! Nightcrawlers and earthworms. Shiny, slippery worms and worms that were asleep. There must have been a thousand worms. No, a million worms. No, it must be a *thousand million worms*!

Mr. Weaver started to laugh. Jody liked to see Mr. Weaver laugh. Mr. Weaver would roll his head back and laugh until he shook all over. "Ha! Ha! No, Jody," Mr. Weaver laughed, "probably not *that* many. But a lot. You can never have enough worms, you know." Jody couldn't imagine needing worms.

Mr. Weaver had a beautiful garden. There were flowers from Africa and China, bright daisies, and sunflowers as big as Jody. Everyone said it was because Mr. Weaver had a green thumb. Mr. Weaver said it was because he had wonderful dirt. To have wonderful dirt, he insisted, you need lots of worms. The job God gave worms was to keep dirt fresh and loose. "Plants like worms," Mr. Weaver said, and smiled.

Mr. Weaver sat down under a great big tree. "Jody, do you remember the story Jesus told about dirt?" Mr. Weaver began. "One day a man was planting seed. He was walking through a field and throwing a handful of seed into the air. Some of the seeds fell where he was walking, and the birds ate them. Some fell where there were too many rocks and couldn't grow well. Some fell where there were weeds. But some fell in good dirt, and they grew strong."

Mr. Weaver reached down and grabbed a handful of good, rich dirt. "Let's pretend that my garden is you, Jody. God wants your life to grow beautiful things: things like love and happiness, good things like friendship and honesty. God wants them to grow. We help God by making our lives good place to grow things. God helps us do that."

"What about worms?" Jody asked with a laugh. Mr. Weaver began to laugh and shake all over. "No, Jody. Worms are only for real gardens."

Kweisi and the Two Houses

 want to tell you a story," Kweisi's (Kwee-see) grandfather said. Kweisi's grandfather was called Boto (Bow-tow), and he was old and wise. "See if you can tell me what it means."

Kweisi was thinking about running in the grass and making circles around trees, but he stopped to listen. Boto said, "One day Jesus was talking to a lot of people. Jesus told them about a man who wanted to build a house. This man built his house on a rock. There was another man who built his house on sand. Then it began to rain. And the wind blew hard." Kweisi's grandfather bugged out his eyes and filled his cheeks with air and blew hard. "It rained so much that the creeks flooded." His voice became quiet. "When it was over, the house on the rock still stood tall and strong, but the house on the sand had fallen down. Jesus said, 'If you listen to me and do what I ask you to do, you are like the house built on the rock.' What does Jesus' story mean?"

Kweisi thought and thought. And then he thought *hard*. And then he sat on a rock so that he could think *really hard*. He jumped up, ran a circle around a tree, and then just stood there. He didn't know. He couldn't guess. He made a sad face even though he wasn't sad. He was hoping his grandfather would see.

Boto took Kweisi's hand and they walked to a big tree with many branches. On one side was a big, strong branch. On the other side was a branch that wasn't strong. Boto lifted Kweisi up so that

he could reach the big branch. Kweisi swung on the branch. He kicked his feet in the air. It felt good. He laughed. Boto lifted him down and carried him to the weak branch. This time he held tight to Kweisi's legs.

Kweisi grabbed the branch, and the branch broke. Kweisi's grandfather said, "The branch that broke is like the house built on the sand. The strong branch is like the house built on the rock."

Boto held Kweisi tight in his arms and said, "Jesus loves you just as I love you. We want you to be safe. If you listen to stories of Jesus and do what Jesus says, when hard times come you will find it easier to be strong — just like the house that was built on the big rock. Or like swinging on a strong limb."

Kweisi smiled and put his arms around his grandfather.